Don't Wake Up Tiger!

Britta Teckentrup

Britta Teckentrup (signature)

nosy crow

Shhh!

Tiger is fast asleep and we **mustn't** wake her up.

Z Z z

But she's **completely** in the way!
Whatever will the animals do?

They're in such a hurry and they've
got a **big** bunch of balloons to carry, too.

Oh dear,

it's going to be **very** tricky!

How will they get past
without waking her up?

Luckily, Frog has had a **very** good idea.

Frog is using his balloon to float over Tiger.

Well done, Frog!
But we need to make sure Tiger stays asleep.

Can you help?

Swoosh!

Let's **stroke** her nose.

That *always* works.

Ah, good.

Tiger is **still** sound asleep and now it's Fox's turn.

But look! Fox is too heavy for his balloon,
and the balloon is dropping lower and lower.

Blow! Blow as hard as you can!

Pfft!

Well done, Fox and
well done, you!

It's Tortoise's turn now.
But he's looking a bit worried
and I'm not surprised
– Tiger is **waking up!**

Let's **stroke** Tiger's tummy.

There, nice and gentle.
That will help her sleep.

Well done, Tortoise. And thank you!
We couldn't have done it without you.
But now it's Mouse's turn and – **look!**
She's let go of her balloon.

Oh no!

She's falling right onto . . .

. . . Tiger's head!

Uh-oh!

Let's **sing** a lullaby!
And can you **rock** the book, too?
Everyone knows that tigers
love to be rocked to sleep.

Phew,

that was close, wasn't it?

Stork is the very last animal to cross.
Isn't it **lucky** she has such nice, long legs?

But be **careful**, Stork!

Look out for the **balloon . . .**

Oh dear. Tiger is

wide awake!

But now it's time for . . .

. . . Tiger's birthday surprise!

Happy Birthday, Tiger!

Can you sing Happy Birthday, too?

To Oskar
– B.T.

First published in 2016
by Nosy Crow Ltd
The Crow's Nest,
10a Lant Street
London SE1 1QR
www.nosycrow.com

ISBN 978 0 85763 719 2 (HB)
ISBN 978 0 85763 720 8 (PB)

Nosy Crow and associated logos
are trademarks and/or
registered trademarks of
Nosy Crow Ltd.

Text and illustration © Britta Teckentrup 2016

The right of Britta Teckentrup to be identified
as the author and illustrator of
this work has been asserted.

A CIP catalogue record for this book is available
from the British Library.

Printed in China by Imago

Papers used by Nosy Crow are made from
wood grown in sustainable forests.

1 3 5 7 9 8 6 4 2 (HB)
1 3 5 7 9 8 6 4 2 (PB)